Dragon Flies a Kite

by Margaret Hillert
Illustrated by Jack Pullan

NORWOOD HOUSE PRESS

The **Dear Dragon** series is comprised of carefully written books that extend the collection of classic readers you may remember from your own childhood. Each book features text focused on common sight words. Through the use of controlled text, these books provide young children with abundant practice recognizing the words that appear most frequently in written text. Rapid recognition of high-frequency words is one of the keys for developing automaticity which, in turn, promotes accuracy and rate necessary for fluent reading. The many additional details in the pictures enhance the story and offer opportunities for students to expand oral language and develop comprehension.

Shannon Cannon

Shannon K. Cannon, Ph.D.
Literacy Consultant

Norwood House Press • P.O. Box 316598 • Chicago, Illinois 60631
For more information about Norwood House Press please visit our website at
www.norwoodhousepress.com or call 866-565-2900.
Text copyright ©2015 by Margaret Hillert. Illustrations and cover design copyright ©2015
by Norwood House Press, Inc. All rights reserved. No part of this book may be reproduced
or utilized in any form or by any means without written permission from the publisher.

This book was manufactured as a paperback edition. If you are purchasing this book as
a rebound hardcover or without any cover, the publisher and any licensors' rights are
being violated.

Paperback ISBN: 978-1-60357-709-0

The Library of Congress has cataloged the original hardcover edition with the following
call number: 2014030276

This paperback edition was published in 2015.

305R—052017
Printed in ShenZhen, Guangdong, China.

What is that?
What do you have there?
What is that red and orange thing?
Is it something to play with?

Oh, yes.
It is something to play with,
but it needs wind to make it go.

I will show you.

Run, run, run, and
help it go up.

It is going up!
It is going up!

Oh, oh.
Dragon is going up too!
You are way, way up Dear Dragon.
Look down, look down.
What do you see down here?

Can you see the house?
Can you see Mother and Sister?

Can you see our school?
Do you see the blue car?

Do you see the farm?
Do you see the horse?

Do you see the river?
Do you see a boat in the river?

Do you see the nest in the tree?
Do you see baby birds in the nest?

Look out!
Look out!
Look out for the tree!

Oh, oh.
Now you are in the tree.

We can get Dear Dragon down.

Dear Dragon is alright.
But the kite is not good.
We will get a new kite.

Yes, we will need a new kite.

Oh, Dear Dragon.
It is good to have you down.

Here you are with me.
And here I am with you.
Oh what a good day, Dear Dragon.

WORD LIST

Dear Dragon Flies a Kite uses the 71 words listed below.
The **7** words bolded below serve as an introduction to new vocabulary, while the other 64 are pre-primer. You may wish to write the words on index cards and use them to help your child build automatic word recognition. Regular practice with these words will enhance your child's fluency in reading connected text.

a	farm	kite	red	way
alright	for		**river**	we
am		look	run	what
and	get			will
are	go	make	school	**wind**
	going	me	see	with
baby	good	Mother	**show**	
birds			**Sister**	yes
blue	have	need(s)	something	you
boat	help	**nest**		
but	here	**new**	that(s)	
	horse	not	the	
can	house	now	there	
car			thing	
	I	oh	to	
day	in	orange	too	
Dear	is	our	tree	
do	it	out		
down			up	
Dragon		play		

ABOUT THE AUTHOR

Photograph by Glenna Washburn

Margaret Hillert has written over 80 books for children who are just learning to read. Her books have been translated into many different languages and over a million children throughout the world have read her books. She first started writing poetry as a child and has continued to write for children and adults throughout her life. A first grade teacher for 34 years, Margaret is now retired from teaching and lives in Michigan where she likes to write, take walks in the morning, and care for her three cats.

ABOUT THE ADVISOR

Dr. Shannon Cannon is a teacher educator, in the School of Education at UC Davis where she also earned her Ph.D. in Language, Literacy, and Culture. Currently, she serves on the clinical faculty supervising pre-service teachers and teaching elementary methods courses in reading, effective teaching, and teacher action research. Her own research interests include; early literacy, research-based reading instruction, English learners, culturally responsive teaching, "funds of knowledge" perspectives, neuroscience, social emotional learning, and project-based learning. Shannon began her career in education teaching elementary-aged children in a year-round school. Subsequently, she spent over 15 years in educational publishing developing and writing curricular programs and providing professional development support to classroom teachers across the country.

ABOUT THE ILLUSTRATOR

A talented and creative illustrator, Jack Pullan, is a graduate of William Jewell College. He has also studied informally at Oxford University and the Kansas City Art Institute. He was mentored by the renowned watercolor artists, Jim Hamil and Bill Amend. Jack's work has graced the pages of many enjoyable children's books, various educational materials, cartoon strips, as well as many greeting cards. Jack currently resides in Kansas.